Ilse

I

"HOW beautiful it is this morning!" Ilse cried, and she jumped out of bed, her little feet looking like two pink birds against the black wood of the attic floor. "How beautiful it is!" and she ran to the window and flung it open.

The sun was everywhere. It lay upon the river and played with the little waves. It was only five o'clock, but already everything was bright and shining, as if someone had spent the entire night furbishing up the little houses, the bridges and the trees, and especially the beautiful yellow sunflowers.

It was already warm, and the chattering of the happy birds all about was making a shrill uproar.

Ilse leaned out of the window and gazed in delight at the pretty sight that Bamberg presented. She lived on the right bank of the river, quite at the end of the village, and she could see the outline of the Rathaus, which filled the center of the horizon.

The irregular cottages that bordered the Main here made it look like an admirable etching by Whistler. Ilse's house was the most notable of them; it quite looked as if it were there only for its picturesque effect and not at all to be lived in. It was all black, with a little projecting black roof over a balcony that projected too, and underneath, jutting out into the water, there was a narrow strip of land in which on either side of the tiny door grew immense sunflowers; their yellow heads reached almost to the balcony, and the little windows of this doll-house seemed scarcely larger than the flowers.

Ilse was seventeen. She lived with her brother, Hans Turner, a fine-looking young fellow, as brown as a Ribera, who four years before had married Katherine, the daughter of his neighbor, Peter. They had one little child, called Richard after Wagner, whose fame was making the fortune of the country.

Ilse was very pretty, no one could deny that; she looked as if she were made of flowers, for her eyes were like violets and her hair was the color of the sunflowers about her cottage. She was as white as the white bindweed, with a faint tinge of pink in her cheeks; she was tall, slender and supple; she had an adorable figure and surprising grace. Indeed, she seemed like a little princess.

Ilse was happy. She had never known a sorrow, and the idea that anyone might be unhappy had never occurred to her. Everybody loved her, and she loved everybody. Everybody was good—she could not believe that there were any wicked people. She was very sorry for the little fishes that were caught in the nets, but she had been brought up in the midst of fishermen and knew that their death was an unavoidable necessity.

Her brother did not require her to do any work, for he was very proud of her delicate beauty. Katherine was quite equal to the needs of the household, and so she had nothing to do all day but take care of the little one sometimes and look after the red bullfinch that lived in its cage near the window like a pomegranate flower on the wall. She also spent much of her time with the great yellow sunflowers.

Ilse was very devout, though she had a strange religion. She believed as firmly in the Holy Virgin as she did in the fairies, the *Zwerges* and *Heimelmännchen* that come into poor people's houses at night and do their work for them. She believed in the elves and thought that the flowers had souls. She knew very well that the Holy Virgin loves flowers; for that reason every Saturday she took a sunflower to the little painted statuette at the comer of the Kreuzstrasse. She talked familiarly to the little Jesus, just as she talked to the bullfinch and the flowers. She believed in Paradise and Fairyland, but she never thought of Hell.

She had, too, a particular liking for the equestrian statue of Konrad III in the cathedral. He was very proud and handsome on his stone horse, which had so very little room on its flower-carved pedestal. The horse always looked as if it were on the point of falling; one could not understand how, being so full of life, he could stay up there so skillfully balanced, on that narrow place. But the proud emperor, with his head thrown back and his lips curling so disdainfully, seemed to care little for that; he held his bridle with a firm hand and looked defiantly into the depths of the cathedral, and his brows frowned and his nostrils dilated. Ilse adored him; he did not inspire her with the least fear, in spite of his imperious air; she thought he saw wicked dragons in the air, like that of the Angel Michael, and that he was justly angry at them. She used to go and talk to him, telling him the little happenings of her life, and then, as she could not reach up to him, she would leave flowers on the stone floor before him as offerings.

She lived a peaceful and simple life that flowed along as evenly and as untroubled as the river that ran before her door.

II

AT the side of the Rathaus lived Heinrich Rothkeppel. He was a spice merchant in comfortable circumstances. He had a great love for flowers, and cultivated roses in a little patch of land. This ridiculous garden, of only a few square yards, overhung the water in front of the astonishing structure that juts out into the water like an excrescence of the Rathaus.

When evening came and his daily work was finished he went down to care for the flowers in his garden. He would put on a straw hat and go out with a very important air, with his pruning shears in his hand. He examined the bushes, looking very carefully at each flower, holding them up between his fat fingers with an extreme care that was touchingly and grotesquely maternal. He cut off the parasitic shoots and the dead leaves that saddened him, for they were like wrinkles on the faces of his flowers, forerunners of old age and death. He killed the caterpillars, too, with an angry air, feeling a just indignation against these mischievous pests. But his greatest joy was to graft a white rose on a red rosebush.

All the flowers were carefully grouped according to their kinds in little beds that were close together and grotesquely imitated clumps of trees. Perfect order reigned there; it was like a doll's garden carefully and systematically kept. Between the triangle that formed the center of the garden and the narrow paths that bordered it Rothkeppel had constructed a ridiculous little path. In it he had strewn clean gravel in which small particles of crystal glittered like diamonds. On the wall, almost down to the water's edge, wild grapes hung, and glycines like great yellow bees, and orange and golden nasturtiums. On the side toward the road, which formed the base of the triangle, the wall overhung the garden.

Heinrich Rothkeppel was thirty years old. He was a sturdy fellow, with honest blue eyes, as blue as bits of delft, and hair as yellow as a canary's breast. He was stubborn and gentle, timid and without malice, phlegmatic, a little slow and something of a dreamer, and his mind was ruminative. He was accounted a good match, for his business was prosperous and the entire house on the corner facing the Rathaus belonged to him; his name could be read in great black letters on its façade above the first story.

Rothkeppel was the ideal of the young women of Bamberg. Their little hearts beat for him in secret, and on St. Sylvester's day, when they dropped melted lead into water to learn the secret of their fate, they all hoped to see the metal assume the shape of Rothkeppel's portrait or initials.

The most persistent in this matrimonial dream was Lina Minniglich, who kept the little notions shop across the street. She was as pretentious as her name, astonishingly tall and bony, and without the least physical attraction.

She considered herself very superior, for while
a *Dienstmädchen* at Munich she had learned
a few words of French and English from the
servants of the families for whom she worked.
She was extremely proud of her learning and
displayed it on every occasion. She owned a
little shop on the other side of the street, opposite Rothkeppel, in which a strange miscellany
of articles were sold: sugar plums and thread,
raisins and tobacco, linen, stockings, candy
and boots, combs, wine, spectacles and rat poi-
son—even an old bathtub and a few porcelain
cups. She was particularly proud of dealing
in gloves, which was not a thriving business,
for gloves are worn scarcely at all at Bamberg;
but she felt infinitely superior to all the village
on account of her "assortment," which was
never broken, and the colors of which, chosen
by herself, were wonderful and startling. She
called herself a "glover," considering that title
very distinguished. On a large placard, written
in large red letters with many faults of spelling,
these words could be read:

Beneath this was written in apple-green letters: "Je barle vran ez," and beneath this again in plain yellow: "Inglesh spokken."

Lina Minniglich was forty years old and confessed to thirty; she wore her hair in girlish ringlets about her neck; she was very rich and prodigiously avaricious. She had set her cap for Heinrich Rothkeppel, her neighbor across the way, not only because he was a desirable match, but because this sturdy, easygoing, gentle fellow greatly pleased the old maid. Having worked hard all her life, a thirst for love suddenly began to rage furiously in her. Her instinctive desire for property and her love for domination fell in with this new feeling, for in this projected marriage there were elements to gratify them both.

Leaning her face against the pane, behind her tricolored placard, Lina watched Heinrich Rothkeppel. She followed his goings and comings, and in the evening when the weather was fine she would put on a pair of gloves and go across to the parapet. Then she contemplated the amateur gardener's home with wistful eyes, but Rothkeppel, absorbed in his work, took no notice of her. The old maid would cough discreetly. Rothkeppel paid not the least attention. She coughed again, and then all at once would say, "*Guten Abend, Herr Nachbar.* It is a beautiful evening. How are your roses getting on?"

"Good evening, Frau Lina," he would reply, raising his head. "Yes, it is fine weather, and my roses are doing very well." Then he would imperturbably return to his plants, snipping off the dead leaves that annoyed him. After a few minutes he would lightly raise his hat and go into the house, for Lina Minniglich bored him.

She was wasting her time in vain hopes, and so were the young girls of Bamberg, for Heinrich Rothkeppel had already made his choice.

III

ONE Sunday as he was tending his plants, Heinrich, happening to raise his head, saw leaning on the parapet a young girl who was looking at him. She was fair and very beautiful and suggested all kinds of flowers. He stood staring at her open-mouthed, astonished at the contrast she made to the shopkeeper he was accustomed to find there.

The girl smiled and bowed to him prettily. He raised his hat awkwardly, and then, after a moment's silence, asked: "Do you love flowers?"

"Oh, yes, I love flowers," she replied, her pretty face lighting up with pleasure.

"Would you like to come in and see my garden?" he asked hesitatingly.

19

"Oh, yes, indeed I would!" she cried enthu-siastically, as if she had been invited to visit Paradise.

He was flattered. "Wait," said he, "I will go around and show you the way," and he went into the house, emerging presently by the door that gave on the street.

"Come," said he, and she followed him.

Then he gravely showed her the plants, explaining their various characteristics. "This one, you see, is very rare, it is very little culti-vated here. This gloxinia comes from Munich, and this marsh-trefoil from the neighborhood of Starnberg."

The girl said nothing; she only looked with all her eyes.

She stopped before a velvety rose, and, pointing to the flower, asked, "May I kiss it?"

"Yes, you may do so," he replied solemnly, as if he were conferring a great favor.

She leaned over and kissed the rose. He looked at her wistfully, and then, "You have no flowers at home, have you?" he asked pity-ingly, in the same tone in which he would have asked her if she had nothing to eat at home.

"I have only sunflowers," she replied. "We have no room to grow anything else."

He reflected for a moment and then suddenly came to a bold decision. "Would you like to have that flower?" he asked.

She looked at him speechlessly to see if he were not joking; and then an incredible thing happened: Rothkeppel cut off a flower that was not yet faded!

She took the flower and looked at it as the town girls look at jewels in the shop windows. "Thank you," she said, "you are very kind."

He was profoundly moved. "Where do you live?" he asked.

"Down there," she replied, pointing in the direction of the river.

"What is your name?" he asked again.

"Ilse," she replied.

"It is a pretty name," he remarked, and led her back to the street. "You may come again to gather flowers whenever you like," he said as he left her.

And in his heart he decided that he would marry Ilse.

Not long after this he made Hans's acquaintance, but as Ilse was very young it was decided that the marriage should be put off until winter had come.

IV

IT was eleven o'clock, and the day was un-
bearably warm. However, a stranger stood
on the bridge behind the Rathaus, looking
curiously about him. He was very tall and
perhaps a trifle slender, but he had handsome,
delicate features, and long, fine eyes, whose
peculiarity and charm lay in their downward
slant, the direct contrary of Mongolian eyes.
His thin lips were beautifully shaped, indicat-
ing a certain weakness and much irony. He
was clean-shaven in the English fashion that is
so becoming to regular features. His complexion was very dark, as if he were permanently
tanned. His father being Italian and his mother
an Irishwoman, he possessed the great charm
that often results from the mingling of races.

He was a looker-on. He loved the arts passionately, but he practiced none of them with any considerable success, a result rather of his extreme indifference and versatility than of a lack of natural gifts. He was very handsome and very much petted, but that did not suffice him. He had a melancholy soul that was at once enthusiastic and disillusioned. He was not capable of any sustained effort nor of continuity in his ideas. He was not good, nor was he bad; he was an idler, that is all. He idled through life and recognized his own uselessness.

He had just returned from Bayreuth, where Wagner's art had delighted and then saddened him, for it had made him feel once more his inferiority, his impotence to create and the futility of his efforts. This was a great sorrow to him; but still he could never find the necessary energy and determination to be great in anything that he undertook.

There, as everywhere, he had met pretty and amiable women; but as he had never had anything but successes in this line, they no longer attracted him, and he had not respond-

ed to the flirtatious advances of a very pretty
Spanish woman whom Wagner's music seemed
to dispose to tenderness. Disgusted, bored and
somewhat irritated, he had wandered as far as
Bamberg. Someone had told him, during an
entr'acte of the "Meistersinger," that he must
see this little village, and, though he never
followed the ideas or counsels of others, he
decided that he would go there. The name
having pleased him, he suddenly and without
any definite reason had left Bayreuth.

It had been very warm in the train, and
he had thought it stupid to travel in such
hot weather, but the appearance of Bamberg
enchanted him at once. He found it an incomparable town; its unexpected prettiness
surprised him with a little shock of contented
astonishment. He was so absolutely charmed
with it that he resolved to stay there until
the next day, in spite of the heat, in order to
make a sketch of the Rathaus, which is set on
a bridge fairly in the middle of the river, and
is covered with colored frescoes like a faded
flowered robe.

Leaning on the bridge opposite, he looked at it; it seemed to him to look like a little Noah's Ark for very little children, this mite of a house set astride the pile-work of the Rathaus, which stuck out like the keel of a ship. He found it funny, naive and ridiculously pretty, and he smiled with amusement at the triangle of garden that bordered the river on the left in an unexpected and picturesque fashion, like an enormous bouquet set down there.

As he gazed at the scene, he saw two men in a flat-bottomed boat. They had great difficulty in keeping it in place because of the eddy made by the great wheel of the mill, and from time to time they cast a net in the river. They stood upright and directed the boat with long poles.

Suddenly he was filled with a desire to go out on the water. He hailed the men, but they paid no attention to him, his voice being drowned by the sound of the mill-wheel. Then, frowning, with the comers of his mouth drawn down angrily, he went down to the bank of the river. He could brook no opposition.

"Twenty marks for you," he said, "if you will take me aboard your boat." The men heard him at once and came alongside. They laid an oar across the thwarts in order that he might sit on it.

The craft glided out on the Main, past the Rathaus and under the bridge, and then drifted slowly down before the Whistlerian houses. Gently the boat slipped by the pretty little irregular houses, and the river sparkled beneath the burning sun.

Satisfied with his whim, the stranger looked about him with a careless pleasure that was full of vague contempt. All at once he sat up, his attention suddenly aroused. He beheld a little black house with a balcony before it, and in front of this house, between two rows of sun-flowers of an intense, violent, crude yellow, a young girl was standing. She wore a gown of forget-me-not blue, and in her arms she held a child in a red dress. The colors stood out sharply against the black background, and the picture was so perfectly composed of harmoni-ous and striking tones that he was enchanted with it, for he took as great delight in colors as he did in sound.

Fascinated at first by the colors, he stared at the pretty picture, and then all at once he was filled with boundless astonishment at the fine grace of the girl. Surely she could not be a fisher's daughter. He looked with delight at her sunny hair, her big tranquil eyes, and her astonishing complexion, but more than all these her perfectly harmonious grace attracted him. The child, which she held in her arms with such an astonishing perfection of pose, was pretty, too, with its blond ringlets.

Old stories ran through his mind, stories in which princesses go about disguised as servants. "Goldenhair must have looked like that," he thought.

Artist as he was at bottom, he found a delicious pleasure in this perfect picture. While he was gazing at it, the fishermen had drawn nearer in order to get aboard from a moored boat to set across the thwarts so that the stranger might be more comfortably seated.

"Is that your house?" he asked, full of a singular content.

"Yes, that is my house," the fisherman replied.

The stranger congratulated the man on his superb sunflowers. The man looked at him with a surprised air. What could there be to admire in those very ordinary, common flowers? But he said politely, "If the flowers please you, you may have some of them." Then he cried out to the young girl: "Ilse! Throw some sunflowers into the boat."

Ilse still stood motionless with her eyes fixed on the stranger, who with a certain delicacy quickly protested. "No, no, do not destroy them, I would rather see them close by."

"As you like," the man answered, and he drew the boat up alongside the sunflowers.

Ilse had not moved. She still stared at this young man, whose beauty surpassed her dreams. Whence could this stranger have come? Surely he must be a prince. His long, slanting eyes were fastened on hers.

"Come, come; what is the matter with you, that you stand there like a stick?" Hans asked with impatient bruskness.

But the stranger bowed courteously; he saluted her as he would have saluted a duchess, and then in his beautiful, gentle voice, he said: "Pardon me, mademoiselle; these sunflowers, whose guardian fairy you seem to be, have drawn me to you from afar."

With an incomparably graceful and supple movement she set the child on the ground and then gravely bowed her head, an exquisite flush mounting to her white face.

"You are welcome," she said, and her voice was like sweet music.

This bored man, who had disdained a famous aristocratic beauty at Bayreuth, now experienced a lively interest—for it was certainly a most unexpected occurrence to find such striking distinction in a child of the people.

He cast about in his mind for some excuse for remaining.

"First let me pay what I owe you," he said pleasantly, handing the promised twenty-mark piece to Hans. "But I would love to make a sketch of your pretty home. May I sit here?" and he pointed to the moored boat.

"If you care to paint my humble house," Hans replied courteously, "I shall be most happy." In this family they all had a certain innate grace. "If you'll allow me," he added, "I shall return to my fishing. Ilse, give the gentleman whatever he desires."

Then Hans shoved off his boat and went back to his fishing behind the Rathaus.

The stranger drew a little sketchbook from his pocket. Ilse was still looking at him. It seemed to her that something had been born within her. She looked at his wavy brown hair, his large drooping gray eyes, and his perfect mouth; at one moment she thought of an angel, of the Angel Michael or Saint George, and at another of the Fairy Prince.

He allowed her plenty of time to satisfy her curiosity, and then he looked at her. He looked at her, sure of his power, with the almost feminine coquetry that was one of his qualities and made him almost irresistible; and all at once it occurred to him that it would be a very agreeable pastime to charm this little girl and give a brief interest to his life.

In a few minutes he had made a rapid sketch. Silent and erect, Ilse looked at him, separated from him only by a narrow line of water. She had never seen any men other than Hans and Heinrich Rothkeppel and the citizens of Bamberg, and a few eccentric Englishmen who passed through; now she was petrified with admiration, and under the influence of his dangerous looks her innocent heart went completely out to him without her being aware of it.

"How thirsty I am!" he exclaimed, rising when he had finished his sketch. "Will you give me some water?" He had a caressing voice, the voice of a petted child who is begging for something. He had tempting eyes. Setting his foot on the ground he asked, "May I see your home, Fraulein Ilse?"

She nodded her head. Her heart was beating; a strange joy had swept over her, and at the same time an unknown fear, for he deigned to enter her house!

V

HE stayed there all the afternoon, making her talk and telling her a thousand insignificant and pretty, trifling stories. She showed him her treasures—her red bullfinch and her sunflowers—and he learned her funny little beliefs.

He was charmed and almost saddened. Not once was his very exacting taste offended, for she betrayed none of the uglinesses of poverty—she had the manner of a little princess, and even her poor little house was so picturesque and pretty that it suggested a very esthetic scene in a theatre.

He did not touch her, for he saw such a pretty little soul in her blue eyes. But then that was not what he wanted; he simply wanted to win her pure heart, that was all; and, in fact, he was in no great hurry to go, for the performances at Bayreuth were to last for three weeks more, and this little bird's soul in a flower-body interested him very differently from the Duchess of Toledo. Yes, he would stay for a few days in this picturesque Bamberg, and he would paint the portrait of this little sunflower girl. He would never again find so perfect a model, and then it would be a pretext to give the brother.

When Hans returned he told him his idea, which did not surprise the brother, for painters were no rare sight in Bamberg. The citizens were accustomed to seeing them come and go, making pictures of everything they found by the way, of a heap of stones, of flowers, of a tree, of a sheep, of all sorts of common and absurd things. Ordinarily they were poor, slovenly, long-haired and far from open-handed. But that made no difference; this unusual painter, who had the good taste to choose Ilse for his model instead of a goose or pig, had none of the faults of his kind, that was all.

"Your sister is as pretty as a flower. She has the air of a little princess," the stranger had said, and that had won Hans's simple heart.

For the first time in her life Ilse could not sleep. Ordinarily she got into her little bed very quickly; but this evening she undressed slowly, and there were dreams in her big eyes.

A great, unknown joy had entered into her; it seemed to her that the queen of the fairies had sent her a message. Everything was vague and confused in her mind, but everything was changed; she no longer felt that she was the same little girl who had got up that morning so care-free, so ignorant of happiness and still so glad to be alive amid the shrill music of the birds.

Ilse could not sleep. Now the moon came in through the window and bathed her in its pale rays. She sat down on her little bed, clasping her arms about her knees, and stared into space with unseeing and ecstatic eyes. Love had entered her heart, and she did not understand its wonderful magic that is so gentle, so radiant, so mysterious and so sad.

She got up and looked at the moon that swam in the heavens, placid, benevolent and friendly. There was not a cloud in the sky, and on the river lay a broad band of shimmering silver like a white road in a dark field.

"How beautiful it is!" she murmured, crossing her arms on her breast. "How good God is!"

And at last, toward morning, she fell asleep.

VI

THE sun poured in through the window. Ilse opened her great violet eyes, and all at once, in the confusion of awakening, she thrilled with joy at the happiness that had come to her.

When Hans had gone out to his fishing she hurried downstairs to see the stranger from a distance when he would come out on the river. She shielded her eyes from the sun with her hand, without suspecting how marvelous she was, standing thus, and with beating heart she waited.

He came at last. He was carefully dressed, in the becoming négligé that young men wear during the summer. In his hand he held some yellow roses. "Good morning, Mademoiselle

Ilse," he called to her gaily. "I have brought you some roses."

"Oh, thank you!" she murmured, looking at him with dazed gratitude. "How good you are!"

He made her take down her hair. She had admirable hair, soft and long and of a beautiful color. He wanted to paint her standing among the sunflowers, as he had seen her for the first time; only she was not to have the child in her arms.

"May I know your name?" she asked anxiously, all at once, while he was painting.

"I am called Brian," he replied. "Call me Brian."

"Is that your name?" she asked.

"Yes, my baptismal name," he replied. "Why do you wish to know my name?"

She flushed a little, and then replied simply: "I wanted to tell your name to the good God. He has so much to do, you know, that He might make a mistake." As she spoke her eyes were very gentle and serious, and her voice was grave.

He looked at her with a strange look. "So what is your name?" she said.

"I am called the Prince of Trevi," he replied gravely; "but for you I am Brian, just Brian."

She stared at him. So he was really a prince; she had not been mistaken! There was a great light in her heart; the Fairy Prince had come!

That evening, when she had undressed, she brushed her hair with great care. Then she kissed the yellow roses and laid them on her pillow.

"Oh, dear Child Jesus," she prayed before she went to sleep, "take good care of him. He is called the Prince of Trevi, and he is stopping at the Inn of the Blue Goose. You cannot make a mistake. I know well that you are very busy, with all the sick people and the afflicted and the prisoners and the orphans, too; but take care of him just the same, and do not let the good fairies ever leave him. You will not forget, dear, good God, will you? And in order that you may be contented I will take my silver cross to your cathedral, which should please you." Then she fell asleep with a smile on her face.

VII

THE next day he came again.

And this day, too, passed for her in a dream of happiness. She gave no thought to what was to come in the future. It seemed to her miraculous that he, this stranger from Fairyland, should deign to come to her and should find pleasure in painting her. For Ilse he was sacred, inscrutable and distant as a god. He came from the land of the fairies, and surely their gentle queen had sent him.

Brian talked to Ilse and told her stories in his own peculiar way, which was dreamy, cynical and poetical, half artificial and half sad, like his own character.

And she told him the things she dreamed—pretty, simple and touching visions—absurd and impossible things, but always pretty and never vulgar, and sometimes very wise things, of a strange and mysterious wisdom.

Carried away by her happiness, Ilse talked on unconscious of herself—with, however, a little vague sadness, the latent sadness that is in all fine souls, like the prescience of the end of all things.

With the strange power of fascination that was his, Brian de Trevi became also the brother's friend. As he took him back in his boat in the evening, Hans told him of his projects, of his dream of marrying his sister to Heinrich Rothkeppel; but she was too young yet to marry, and so they had decided to say nothing to her until the next winter.

VIII

"IT is really too fine to paint this morning," cried Brian in his fresh, young voice. "Come instead, and show me your cathedral."

He had the triumphant air of a schoolboy on a holiday. He was as beautiful as a young god, beaming with life and careless gaiety— and he wore a pink shirt.

She looked at him, fairly dazzled. How beautiful he was, and how good, to be willing to go with her to the cathedral!

They passed down before Rothkeppel's garden. Brian stopped and leaned on the parapet. He began to laugh, for Rothkeppel, very red, rather grotesque and ridiculously busy, was pottering about his plants.

"What marvelous flowers there are in that absurd garden!"

Rothkeppel raised his head and turned pale. He had not heard Brian's words, but he knew about the portrait, and he was very much afraid for Ilse.

"Oh, his garden is very pretty," the girl replied, blushing a little from pleasure and uneasiness. "I love it so much."

He looked at her curiously—what was she to this man? Then, lifting his eyes, he saw the name written on the house in large letters. Ah, that, then, was her future husband! He looked at her again, but he could read nothing in her fair eyes. No, she knew nothing of Hans's project, that was evident; but this horticulturist's ambition seemed to him inordinate, and at once his evil designs became intensified, took form; this exquisite flower, formed to ornament an angel's hand, should not be set in the garden of this loutish man.

She walked along with her graceful, elastic step, without a thought of her bare little feet, and he glanced at her out of the comers of his eyes, surprised and charmed by turns at the perfect grace of her movements.

From the other side of the road, concealed by her tricolored placard, Lina Minniglich was on the watch. When the girl passed, with the great bunch of roses in her hand and Brian smiling by her side, her eyes shone maliciously, and she slyly followed them at a distance.

They went into the cathedral. The emperor on his stone horse was staring into the emptiness of the church, his lips curled in disdain and his arrogant eyes defying an invisible enemy, and the imprudent horse, always hovering over the abyss, stood with its feet set on the acanthus leaves.

"There," said Ilse, "that is Konrad III."

But the emperor had an indignant air. It seemed to Brian that he looked particularly at him with an air that was reproachful, displeased, aggressive and disapproving. He was a little ashamed of what he was doing, but he never brooked opposition or even protest, and the silent disapproval of this statue irritated him. He looked at her with an ironical smile that distorted the fine lines of his mouth. "Poor little Ilse!" he said. "If you had not that inoffensive stone knight for a protector, what would become of you?"

She lifted her eyes, surprised and a little troubled, too, by the evil tone of his voice.

"But I am never in any danger, you see," she said vaguely, "and then I'm sure he would protect me. He and the angels, and the dear holy Virgin, and the queen of the fairies—they would protect me always and against everything, of that I am very sure," and in her calm eyes, as in her words, there was a perfect confidence, an absolute and childish faith. It was supremely sad, almost pathetic, for her confidence was so vain.

He looked at her with a smile that had in it a certain pity, and he thought how little they could guard her, these protectors of stone and of her imagination, against her destiny, against himself.

"Shall I go away?" be thought. "Shall I leave her now while there is yet time?" But the memory of Rothkeppel crossed his mind, and an ugly smile disfigured his handsome features. No, that man made it impossible.

Still, he did not love this little girl, with her soft, white feet and her flower-like face— and still less did he desire her; but she was so charming, with her absurd little great ideas, so strange, so unlike the women he had known heretofore, that he could not leave her; and it was at once exquisite, fresh, and new and almost interesting to feel that her reserved, pretty soul was being filled with him, belonged to him completely. And he closed his heart against pity.

What harm was he doing, after all? He would go away, and sooner or later she would marry Rothkeppel; but afterward and always, when eventide came and the stars shone in the sky, when the children had been put to bed and Rothkeppel walked beside her in the garden, all at once she would have a little shiver of disgust and would turn away from him and repulse him; then alone, leaning on the parapet, between the yellow nasturtiums and the purple wistaria, she would dream of Brian a little sadly. Oh, he was sure of that; she would never forget him to the end of her days.

However, how many hearts had he broken already, simply because it had amused and then bored him? But she would not have her heart broken, her gentle, little girl's heart; she would only say simple little prayers for him always. He would be the one memory of her life—that would be all.

Before going out Ilse knelt down without shame or ostentation, very simply, because it was her custom to do so, and, with her clear eyes raised, she prayed.

He remained standing beside her, his hat in his hand, a little saddened.

Presently they went out of the church.

"Ilse, what were you praying for just now?" he asked, stopping all at once.

The pale little face became quite rosy.

"I was praying to God that you might be happy always," she said simply, "and I was thanking Him for the great happiness of having known you."

Something in her words touched him. He took her hand quickly in his and gravely pressed his lips to it.

"If there is a God somewhere," he thought, "this little girl is after His own heart," and he silently accompanied her home while she chattered to him.

"I shall leave tomorrow," he said to himself. "I must leave her in peace."

However, he promised to come and see her that evening and to take her out on the water, for the moon was at the full.

As he was going home to dinner he stepped into a jeweler's shop. He could find nothing there that suited him, so he took off a pearl that he always wore and had it set in a gold ring. It was a beautiful pearl without a flaw.

"I shall go away," he thought. "It would be abominable to remain; but I shall go out with her this evening again, poor little thing."

IX

A GREAT peace lay upon all things. Church bells sounded in the silence, for tomorrow would be the Feast of the Assumption.

Slowly they untied the boat before the black house. The sunflowers were no longer yellow; they were little wheels of pale silver, like ghosts of sunflowers. There was something strangely peaceful, something profoundly calm in the air.

She sat in the stern, for he did not wish her to row. It was as beautiful and unreal as a dream, and a gentle, ecstatic joy nestled in Ilse's heart.

She did not say anything. Her long hair, which was like silver this evening, floated in the warm air. He gazed at her; she looked like a fairy, the fairy whose name she bore. Suddenly he stopped rowing and the boat glided gently along in the moonlight.

It was mild—adorably mild, and not a sound was heard save now and again when the light lapping of the water against the boat sounded like a sob. The silence was almost palpable and permeated with a sombre sadness.

Feeling a little oppressed and seized by a sudden presentiment, Ilse looked at him uneasily; but he averted his eyes and would not meet her glance.

"Ilse," he said, drawing the ring from his pocket, "will you wear this in memory of me when I am gone away?"

She made a frightened movement, and a great terror, a great darkness, descended upon her. She had not thought that he might go away. She gave no attention to the ring, but only repeated, "Gone away?" and her eyes grew wide with fear.

"Yes," he said in a low tone, "I must go." And as she said nothing he continued, "I must go away tomorrow."

In the brilliant light of the moon he could see her face quiver. All at once she stood up; she seemed like some visionary being made of silver—of dark silver on a background of silvery white. She sank at the young man's feet, leaning her head against his knees. "Oh, no, you must not go! Do not go, do not go!" Her eyes were dry and her voice was hoarse. From time to time she repeated, "Do not go, do not go!"

A great pity welled up in Brian's heart. He stroked her hair gently; he tried to raise her up, but she clung to him.

"Oh, stay, stay!" And all the astonishment, the horror of this thought of his departure was in her poor, sad eyes.

All at once she began to weep; great tears flowed slowly down her face. For a moment a sad tenderness that was disinterested and full of pity for this little girl who loved him softened and saddened his heart. He took her in his arms. She nestled in them like a dying child, and he saw on her suffering face a heavenly tenderness, something invincible and divine and mortal that he had never seen before—and yet how many eyes filled with loving tears he had already seen!

Then he bent over her and kissed her on her hair, on her eyes and on her mouth. It was a pure, almost a religious kiss, with neither violence nor passion in it. She was sacred to him, and, though he believed in nothing, he could not profane her. He felt all at once that he was good and wondered at himself, for he was quite sure he would leave her. For an instant the thought came to him, "What if I should take her away?" But immediately her future, the life she would lead when he had tired of her—for he would tire of her, as he had of all the others—was as repugnant to him as a sacrilege. No, he would go away.

Around the boat the water sobbed sadly.

Slowly, as if regretfully, he roused himself and took up the oars. When they reached the house be tied the boat, and then for an instant he hesitated. The house was empty, Katherine and Hans having gone to Neudorf to attend a christening, and a temptation to follow her came over him, a vague desire to possess her, because she was so pretty—and then the pity it would be to do this thing stopped him once again.

He took her in his arms, caressed her hair and kissed her. "Goodbye, Ilse," he said. "Pray for me."

"Shall you come back again?" she asked.

"Yes, I shall come back," he lied.

"When?" she asked. She shivered as if she were freezing.

"I shall come back next year for Bayreuth," he lied again out of pity for her.

She pressed closely to him, weeping silently; but he could find nothing more to say to her.

A light breeze sprang up; clouds swept swiftly across the heavens and hid the moon.

Through the open window a mournful sound came to them; it was the Black Forest clock marking the hour. Twelve times in the silence the wooden cock crowed; it crowed slowly, stupidly and implacably, as if it mocked at destiny. Brian thought that the sound would never cease.

Drops of rain began to fall, large drops that were far apart and warm, and the river lapped uneasily about the house.

"You must go in," Brian murmured. "Good-bye, my darling."

The sunflowers drooped toward the water.

She did not say anything more, she detached her arms from about Brian's neck, she did not try to hold him back, for it was her strange creed that all effort against fate is in vain if one has heard the midnight hour sound in the silence.

Then he went away.

"That is the first sincere love I have ever had," he thought, "and I am going away from it."

In his heart he thought that he was worthy of admiration, as a martyr would be, and he considered that he had done a good deed— only he smiled at himself a little ironically for being so sentimental.

X

WHEN ILSE arose next day, rain was falling in Bamberg. It seemed to her that everything was gone, extinguished, that Brian had taken the sun away with him.

From that day life seemed very sad to her. A single thought sustained her: he would come back, for he had promised. Not for a moment did she doubt him.

All gaiety had gone out of her life. She wandered sadly through the streets. She was pale, and her big, blue eyes looked at the sky.

"What does she see up there that we do not see?" the people whispered among themselves, for she had a strange look in her eyes. But she always saw only a single figure with great, sad eyes that had a downward slant, and a mouth with thin lips that was disdainful and smiling.

Sometimes she closed her eyes; then she felt those thin lips burning on her own.

For hours she would sit in a chair doing nothing. She suffered very much.

She prayed almost all the day. He had said, "Pray for me"; he had asked her to pray for him, and it had become a sacred duty for her, her sole duty.

"Oh, guard him," she said to the Holy Virgin. "Let him have only joy always, and, O Holy Mother, surely it cannot be a sin to implore you that he may come back soon."

She addressed herself, too, to Queen Ilse, her fairy godmother, and to the Emperor Konrad III in the cathedral. And every evening before going to sleep she kissed her white pearl. She went but rarely to Rothkeppel's garden, for the flowers did not seem to understand her. They were as beautiful, as fresh as before, calm, contented and pretty, but they seemed very indifferent. When one suffers much, even the sun seems cruel.

She remained always very much alone in her trouble.

XI

"ILSE!" Lina Minniglich called to her one day. "So your fine lover has gone away!" and she laughed coarsely. "You may be sure he will not come back—they all promise that, these fine gentlemen who come and go."

She raised her pretty, indignant face to the old maid and faced her bravely. "He has promised to come back," she said, "and he will come back." But as she walked along her tears flowed, and for the first time doubt entered her suffering heart.

"Can that horrible thing be, that he will not come back?" But she reproached herself at once for having doubted him for a moment. He had promised—and promises are always kept.

"Heinrich," said Lina Minniglich, leaning over the parapet. "Heinrich, have you noticed how Ilse is pining away since her lover left Bamberg?"

Heinrich laid his pruning shears on the path. A great anger welled up within him and held him paralyzed. He felt himself impotent with rage, full of hatred but powerless before this cruel, wicked woman who had thus touched him to the quick.

As he did not at once reply, she thought she had spoken well, and smiling slyly, she went on:

"Isn't it terrible, Herr Heinrich? Would you believe it, she wears his pearl on her finger—he paid her with that pearl—and she even led her lover into the cathedral! I followed them, dear Herr Heinrich, and I saw them kissing each other. What a sacrilege! Oh, that girl fills me with horror!"

As she spoke she made a scandalized grimace and spread out her hands coquettishly on her breast, displaying her gloves.

Then all at once Heinrich Rothkeppel broke out.

"Woman, be silent!" he thundered, fairly beside himself. "Say no more and go away. If you utter any more of your dirty calumnies, look out for yourself—you understand me?—for I will crush you as I would a mischievous worm."

This gentleman, who always spoke in a low tone, had suddenly developed a terrible voice; he trembled with anger and threatened her with his clenched fist.

The old maid uttered a sharp cry of fear, for this sudden and astonishing outburst in this calm man terrified her. Then tears came to her eyes, tears of rage and envy, for in his anger he seemed to her more handsome, more masculine and desirable than ever, and she knew now with sharp disappointment that her dream was shattered, irremediably destroyed, that he loved Ilse and that never, never would she be his wife.

She cast a vanquished look on her gloves, that now useless luxury. Then, flinging up her hands, she rushed across the street like a crazy woman.

And Heinrich, in his bedroom, wept, with his head in his hands.

XII

"IT is time to speak," Rothkeppel said to Hans when the winter had come.

But when Hans spoke to Ilse she shook her head gently.

"I do not wish to marry," she said. And then Heinrich said to Hans again, "Let us not torment her, poor little thing. She is so young, and it is perfectly natural. Let it be next winter—I can wait."

But his heart contracted. He became very sad and often walked about a little bent, staring at the ground. He neglected his flowers. He knew well that she had done nothing wrong. But he knew, too, that her heart was lost, that her love was given, that it was the handsome, ironical prince who had come and taken it from her; and in his slow brain a fierce hatred grew up against that robber of souls; but greater still was his sorrow for the poor little one whom he saw suffering so. He would have liked to be able to console her, to make her smile, to lessen her burden; but he felt himself absolutely powerless before her sorrow.

And Ilse grew thin and wan.

"You never laugh now," the good Katherine said to her one day. "What is the matter with you? It is only the dead who do not laugh. But you are so quiet, you are too quiet, one would say that you were dead."

XIII

THEN the flowers died.

XIV

WINTER passed and spring came, and with it the flowers and the birds came back, and the sun too—the sun that dances on the little waves and makes the whole world gay. But Ilse's laughter did not come back. She remained cold and pale, for she had wept too many tears. She was calm and brave and absolutely silent.

Oh, would the summer never come again, the summer, with its long, burning days and its beautiful warm nights, the summer that must revive her? Would it not come soon? It was so long, and she was so tired!

Months passed.

She did not know that there were no performances at Bayreuth, that he had lied, had lied twice when he said he would come back. She only thought, "He will soon be here!"

XV

"HOW beautiful it is this morning!" cried Ilse as she jumped out of bed.

The sun was everywhere; it danced on the river and the happy birds made a great to-do.

It was a day just like that on which he had first come, and the resemblance gave her a presentiment of happiness.

Presentiments are almost always deceitful.

Ilse dressed quickly, with a smile in her happy eyes. She carefully brushed her sunny hair, the hair that he loved, and joy brought a tinge of color to her cheeks.

"You look very well this morning," remarked Hans as he kissed his sister. For some months now her pallor had been troubling him, but he had said nothing, not wishing to bother her. But sometimes, when he was

alone, he clenched his hand in terrible anger
at the thought of that stranger who had come
and stolen his sister from him.

"I shall go and visit the emperor," she
thought, in her haste to make the hours pass
quickly, and she set out very busily, with sunshine in her eyes. Heinrich saw her from his
garden.

Silently he glanced at the sky. The recovery
of this sick little soul seemed to him a great
miracle, and his heart was light within him.

"Ilse," he called out to her as she passed, "I
have some roses for you." She smiled on him
with her pretty smile of former days and took
the flowers.

"I shall take them to the emperor," she
thought, "in order that he may guard his coming." Then, almost running in her great haste,
she reached the cathedral.

As she went in she saw that there was a
scaffolding about the statue, for it was being
cleaned; a ladder had been placed against the
scaffolding.

There was no one in the church. In a tavern nearby the workmen were drinking beer.

Ilse looked about her and smiled. "Ah, at last I can get close to him," she sighed; "I can kiss his feet in their armor, and I need not leave my offering on the floor."

What a wonderful day it was to be! Here was one of her great wishes fulfilled, and in a little while her beloved would return!

She climbed up to the feet of the statue. Her yellow hair shone like a monstrance against the gray stones. Her blue cotton gown was like a bit of the sky in the church, and in her hand she held red roses. She laid the flowers among the acanthus leaves, and then, reaching up on tiptoe and leaning against the stone, she reverently kissed the emperor's foot; then she patted the imprudent horse, the amusing horse that always seemed to her so impatient to leap into space.

"Oh, dear emperor," she murmured, clasping her hands, "let him come back to me soon! "As she said these words she lost her balance. For an instant she looked like a great, fantastic bluebird, with her blue skirts fluttering in the air like wings. Without a cry she fell.

There was a short, heavy thud, then mysteriously from all sides of the vast cathedral the echo repeated it. Finally there was a great and oppressive silence; it was as if all things were manifesting their consternation.

Now the sun, striking through the stained-glass windows, covered her with a patchwork of color, innumerable brilliant spots, green, blue, red, yellow and violet. They wove a triumphant garment for her—a fanciful garment that was sewn with gems, a coverlet like a marvelous cloak, like the cloak of a little queen.

For her who had always believed in the unbelievable, mysterious things were done: petals began to fall from the roses laid between the horses' feet, and slowly, like dainty, fairy butterflies, they fluttered capriciously about before alighting, covering her blue robe with a rosy shower. The sunlight caught in her golden hair, making it gleam.

A shade of sadness passed over the aggressive face of Konrad III. Truly, things had more pity than men.

XVI

W HEN the workmen returned from the
tavern they found Ilse lying on the
ground. She seemed to be asleep, lying on her
side there at the foot of the scaffolding.

One of them stooped down to awaken her,
but he started back in fear, for at the comer of
her mouth there was a little spot of red.

Gently they bore her away. There were tears
in their eyes and pity on their rough faces, for
everybody in Bamberg loved this little girl who
was as pretty as a flower.

"She has killed herself because her lover
never came back," one of them remarked pity-
ingly. "Poor little thing!"

And under the huge vault of the church
there was great lamentation, sighs and sobbing
prayers—though reasoning people would have

heard in it only the echo of footsteps that died
away.

They laid her on her narrow little bed.
Outside, the birds were singing joyously and
the river flowed on like a golden stream.
Everything was brutally brilliant with life. It
was one of those days when death seems but
a name.

She opened her eyes and looked curiously
about the room.

She was not suffering, she was only benumbed; there was something heavy, oppressive on her chest.

She looked about her curiously. Beside her
bed she saw Hans standing, sorrowful and
motionless. She did not understand. Vaguely,
without moving, she sought the reason of it all.
Seated beside her bed, Katherine was weeping,
her head in her apron.

Then she remembered.

"Oh, yes, the emperor," she said in a faraway voice. "And then I fell. But it is nothing;
do not cry. Do not cry; I feel quite well."

But while she spoke a little blood still flowed from her mouth.

With a shudder her brother leaned over her. Ilse was silent and smiled with dreamy eyes that did not see him. After a few moments she continued:

"Why do you cry? I am very happy. He is coming, he will be here soon, you know, for he promised me."

Her eyes closed, and in the sun-flooded attic there was a great silence.

Suddenly she drew herself up in the bed with unnatural strength.

"Am I really going to die?" she cried. "Do you believe that I am going to die?"

Great tears streamed down Hans's face. She looked at him for an instant, with the sadness of definite comprehension, and then she went on:

"Well, you see, if I must die it does not matter so much, after all, for I shall go to the good God and His angels. But I think—I *think* I shall hear *his* voice before I die."

A sudden convulsion passed over her face; then when it was gone she said:

"He is coming, I know he is coming. Hans, open the door for him, open the door for him, quickly!"

She sighed, from exhaustion, and, leaning back, seemed to doze.

At the window, the red bullfinch was fairly splitting his throat in his joy in the sunshine.

She opened her eyes once again—she could no longer speak. Only her eyes seemed to be alive now; they were terribly, tragically alive, as though they would speak. They rested on Hans, fixed, anxious and terrible; they spoke, the large, mysterious eyes of one who is almost dead, they clearly asked: "Where is he?"

"He is not here yet," the brother said in a low tone, shaking his head sadly.

She uttered a long, low moan, and into her eyes came a great horror. All at once she understood that he would not come, that he had lied. She knew, all the agony of doubt, at the very moment of dying all her illusions had fallen away.

Nothing had been spared to her before she died.

In the silence there was a little, tragic sound, as faint and heartbreaking as the moan of a bird.

Church bells sounded in the distance. A wandering breeze bore in the perfume of flowers, and the red bullfinch at the window fairly split his throat in the joy of living.

XVII

THE following year a great multitude of diverse people came together for the performances at Bayreuth. By a singular coincidence the *Gazette des Etrangers* published on the same day, side by side, the names of the Prince of Trevi and the Duchess of Toledo. She was stopping with Mme. Krock, a famous and corpulent boarding-house keeper.

Brian, who was lodged in the house of Ries, the tinsmith, was more an idler than ever, more bored, more disgusted, more cynical and more sad. He stared malevolently at the horrible bibelots, the number and incongruity of which were worse than before, and the portrait of Kaiser Wilhelm, gazing down at him from above his bed with its pretty little arrogant air, did not suggest a single thought to him.

The Duchess of Toledo lived opposite. This fair lady, who reproached God for the continued existence of the *Almanach de Gotha*, appeared again, in spite of that irritating index of ages, more beautiful, more painted, more girlish than ever.

But on this occasion Brian succumbed. He was not enthusiastic about the duchess nor was he even the least attracted toward her; but he was in such a state of indifference that to struggle against a passion as determined as hers seemed to him useless and a bore.

Since the woman wanted him with all her strength, very well, she should have him—it really did not matter much; but how tedious, odiously monotonous and false it always was, and why did these silly, importunate, useless and encumbering women always insist on pretending, why were they never jolly girls, but always full of unjustified pretensions and unreasonable exactions?

Ah, it was only music, the divine music of Wagner, that could give one a new sensation. As soon as he had entered the theatre he experienced a sort of nervous exaltation that set his body and soul vibrating.

So a week passed. The Duchess of Toledo began to bore him prodigiously. She was one of those outrageously silly women, but beautiful, with a striking, exotic beauty.

She had an unbearable habit of making remarks to him, which were generally stupid, during the perfonnances. That put him beside himself. Not caring for Wagner's music, to which she preferred Mascagni's, she was supremely bored; but she dissembled her personal opinion out of consideration for the prince's old-fashioned taste.

On the eighth day "Parsifal" was presented. As Trevi, moved by the tremendous emotion of the music, walked about with the duchess after the first act, he looked down at the ground. He walked along mechanically beside her, his heart in a whirl and quite unconscious of her presence.

"Are you looking at my new tan shoes?" she asked him, with a smile. "They are very nice, aren't they? Thomas wrote me that they were exactly like yours."

He raised his eyes and looked at her with a fixed air of surprise; then he left her abruptly and disappeared in the crowd.

"This Brian is a very original fellow," she thought, looking sadly at her new shoes. "What difference does it make to him if I have shoes like his? His monopoly of yellow leather is very curious."

Presently, assisted by one of the young snobs who followed her everywhere, she set out in search of the prince; but neither in the entr'acte nor during the rest of the day did she succeed in finding him.

Next day, as he was annoyed by the strong odor of white lilies that she exhaled, he indulged in some extremely impolite reflections; mature women exasperated him. A great rage rose up within him, an indignant anger against this chattering, flighty, perfumed woman who had forced herself on him.

Then all at once, while Elizabeth's prayer was mounting in the obscurity, something stirred within him. Forgotten scenes returned to him, as if be had suddenly woken up in the morning from a two years' sleep. The touching little girl, Ilse, stood before him, her pitiful face dimmed with tears and an incomparable expression of love in her eyes. On the stage Elizabeth was praying for Tannhauser, but in his ears the voice of Ilse was saying, "May God keep you!"

He found a new sense and a bewildering grace in the delicious words of the legend. A pleasant warmth comforted his heart, a sensation of gentleness, innocence and real tenderness enveloped him, and he felt a strong desire to see Ilse again.

XVIII

THAT same evening he left for Bamberg. As he rolled along in the overheated railway carriage, his ideas were insensibly modified. The blue curtain drawn over the dirty, rattling lamp enclosed his reflections in obscurity, and the two open windows formed a light current of dusty air about him. The train progressed slowly at the heavy pace of a formidable beast in a hurry, and the blinds fluttered desperately, like the wings of captive birds. His thoughts had taken on an anxious cast, and there was a contraction about his heart. Under the evaporation of the excessive heat and the physical discomfort of the hard bench, his enthusiasm insensibly disappeared. Cynical memories effaced his joy and blotted it out as with so many strokes of a pen.

"Ilse must have married Heinrich Rothkeppel," he thought, and the corners of his mouth
drew down mockingly.

"Frau Rothkeppel!" How ugly and vulgar
it sounded. "Rothkeppel, Rothkeppel," he
repeated aloud, amused at the absurd conso-
nance. "There it is," he thought, with a smile.
"I pass my night in an impossible railway
carriage, I travel on the hottest night of the
year, I've left Wagner and the duchess behind,
and all this merely to go and present my com-
pliments to Mme. Rothkeppel." The absurdity
and incongruity of the proceeding seemed so
amusing that he began to laugh.

"Come," thought he, "the *über sich selber
lachen* of the great Nietzsche once more!" This
was one of his favorite theories, which he often
quoted and practiced with a rare complacence.

He continued to laugh at himself with a
disdainful, cynical and easy philosophy. Then
his nervous hilarity passed, and his brain
began to work again. He wondered how his
little sweetheart was getting on. He imagined
her vulgar and commonplace, unrecognizable

with her coarse, red, toil-hardened hands. He thought her complexion must have deteriorated and her figure—her exceptional figure—must have been deformed by maternity. Yes, she had had time to have two children; doubtless she was suckling one now. The thought horrified him. His fastidious taste revolted at the picture; he had never been able to understand the poesy of motherhood, and he felt a scorn for persons who reproduced their kind, for he considered it inartistic, ugly and reprehensible. Sorrow and suffering were the only certain and inevitable things in life, happiness and joy being only relishes, sauces that most people missed, and so by what right did one bring new unfortunates into being?

Then he thought of Ilse's feet, of her perfect, roguish, little feet. They had been like very precious bibelots, delicate, fragile and rare; now they would surely be broken down, dishonored by shoes. "She wears shoes with elastics on the sides now," he thought, making a wry face.

"What a funny idea it was for me to return to Bamberg! It is a mistake for a man ever to go back to the country or the women he has loved. Well, now I am going to destroy a pretty memory, that's all—doubtless much idealized in my mind's eye by the passing of time, a scene and a figure that once delighted me—and I am going to obliterate the delicate picture by the brutal reality of gross ugliness and vulgar banality. Why should I do this foolish thing?"

Then the thought came to him: "What can Ilse be thinking of just now?"

Instead of her graceful ideas, her mysterious and brave little thoughts, she must be thinking only of her kitchen duties and washing the children.

He resolved not to expose himself to the spectacle of the boots with elastics on the sides, but to go away without having seen Ilse again.

XIX

IT was late at night when he reached Bamberg, and there was no train the next day until the afternoon.

"I may as well stroll over to the Rathaus," he thought. "The charm of that old house was so touching that I cannot have been deceived."

The day was very warm. "It is just the same exceptional heat that there was here before," Brian remarked. "From the Rathaus I can see the Rothkeppels' garden; but that doesn't matter, flowers are always pretty, for they come from the land of the fairies."

But when he came to the bridge he was astonished to find that the little garden no longer existed. A few straggling rosebushes and some discouraged plants that had been frozen during the winter flourished sadly alone there, almost choked by the weeds.

"What has happened?" Brian wondered in surprise. "Can Rothkeppel be dead, or does his domestic happiness absorb him to this extent?" He began to laugh, but with a laugh that was not sincere. "No, but what can have come over Rothkeppel that he neglects his garden like this?" It was inexplicable.

He felt a certain regret, however, at the sight of this desolation. He did not like finished or destroyed things, for they excited his melancholy discouragement to an intolerable degree.

"I shall go as far as her house," he thought, "her pretty little black house among the sunflowers," and, seeing some fishermen, he hailed them and floated down the Main.

The boat slipped gently through the water. It passed the Rathaus and the bridges. It passed the houses like Whistler etchings.

And his agitation increased. Perhaps, after all, she was not married and he would see her again, Ilse, the dear little girl, standing among her sunflowers. He hoped that she would wear a blue dress, as she had the first time he saw her.

At last he stood up in order to see more quickly; he shielded his eyes from the sun with his hand. But he could not make out the house.

The boat stopped.

"Is it there that Hans Turner lives?" he asked uneasily.

The men nodded their heads. A sensation of cold glided over his heart, for here, too, the flowers were destroyed. It seemed to him that a wicked magician had passed that way, killing the flowers—all the flowers everywhere in his path, destroying all his memories as a wicked child destroys pretty pictures.

Where the graceful sunflowers had been there were now only dried and weather-beaten stalks, and the house looked like a great black coffin. The black that had been so pretty by contrast now appeared horribly lugubrious, and, as if to emphasize the desolation of the scene, the bullfinch's cage hung on the wall, falling to pieces, with broken bars and empty—it looked like a little skeleton.

XX

HE hesitated a moment before going in; he hesitated on the spot where the great yellow sunflowers had grown, and where, one evening, Ilse had wished to hold him back.

In the house he heard not a sound.

Then a violent desire to flee came over him, to withdraw, never to know; but the door opened, and he found himself face to face with Hans Turner.

The change that had come over the man was eloquent and terrible.

All at once Brian knew, he understood; something unbearable, something crushing had descended upon his heart.

A great surprise came into Hans's face. "Ah, it is you!" he said in a hard tone. "You have come at last! You have come too late."

"Ilse?" Brian asked in a nervous voice, the strange voice of a dying man.

"Ah, you have come now," the other replied, with an angry gesture, "now that she is dead! Go away from here, go away from here!" and as Brian did not answer he thundered at him: "Leave at once, or, by God, I will throw you into the water!"

Brian did not hear him. He did not even see him. A great, silent horror had benumbed him, and he felt only the bitter pain, the overwhelming disappointment of having lost something infinitely precious and irreplaceable. Again he saw distinctly her pale and sorrowful little face—yes, he had promised to return. All that there was in him of sentiment, melancholy and romance suffered keenly.

Hans looked at him and grew more gentle. The sight of this suffering softened him.

"She loved you much," he murmured.

Then almost timidly the prince said: "Tell me of it."

And Hans told him how she had grown paler and paler each day as she waited for

him, and how she had hoped for his return
with never a complaint: he told him that every
day she had prayed for him and that then she
had died with that final despair, that at last she
understood his deception.

When he ceased to speak a heavy silence fell
upon them. There was an incredible intensity,
a terrible finality, in this silence—one would
have said that they would never speak again.

The Black Forest clock squeaked harshly,
and the wooden bird crowed the hour.

Then Hans got up. He brought Ilse's ring
from a chest.

"Take this back," he said. "You see, one
should never give pearls to anyone—pearls are
tears, and they bring bad luck."

XXI

"TAKE me there," said Brian in a low and hoarse voice; and with bowed head Hans showed him the way.

XXII

HER grave was very small; on a cross was to be read only the word "Ilse," with the dates. It was very plaintive, very gentle, this word and these eloquent dates; it was like a little thing that flutters its wings.

Around the cross there was a spell; it was as if all the flowers had taken refuge there, all the flowers that had disappeared from the rest of the world. They had made Ilse's sleep peaceful, they had made a resting-place for her such as she would have wished, for there were great quantities of her dear, beautiful flowers there. They surrounded and quite covered the sad little grave, spreading their fragrance about it and caressing its stones with delicate grace. With their multicolored mouths they seemed to say, when the chattering breeze passed:

"Sleep well, we shall guard you. You are very happy."

And it seemed to Brian that the pretty, childish soul of Ilse sobbed through these flowers.

Poor little girl! It was best that she should rest among these roses, it was best so. On earth she had been, like the flowers and birds and butterflies, joyous and innocent, pretty and without sin. "But the flowers and the butterflies are useless things," say those who are more wise than God. Yes, she had been useless and frail, and pure and beautiful like these things. She had been but a symbol, she had had a soul of crystal.

Poor little Ilse! May she sleep in peace among her flowers, with her fanciful dreams and, who knows? perhaps her dear soul lives again up there and sees the beautiful beings of her dreams; Queen Ilse, and the Emperor Konrad III, and the Holy Virgin, and the seraphim with their diamond wings.

Poor, childish Ilse, it is indeed better that she should sleep. She was only a little girl, life had been too heavy for her. And before she died she had known all the unbearable burden of human suffering. It was very unjust.

The Prince of Trevi felt a strange coldness in his heart. Ah, yes, it was much better that she should sleep, for he could do nothing for her.

"What can one do for anyone?" he thought sadly, and a tear ran down his cheek, a horribly useless tear, for everything is useless.

A perfumed breeze floated by. "Sleep well," said the flowers. "Sleep well, and forget. We know the secret of happiness."

A PARTIAL LIST OF SNUGGLY BOOKS

G. ALBERT AURIER *Elsewhere and Other Stories*
CHARLES BARBARA *My Lunatic Asylum*
S. HENRY BERTHOUD *Misanthropic Tales*
LÉON BLOY *The Desperate Man*
LÉON BLOY *The Tarantulas' Parlor and Other Unkind Tales*
ÉLÉMIR BOURGES *The Twilight of the Gods*
CYRIEL BUYSSE *The Aunts*
JAMES CHAMPAGNE *Harlem Smoke*
FÉLICIEN CHAMPSAUR *The Latin Orgy*
BRENDAN CONNELL *Unofficial History of Pi Wei*
BRENDAN CONNELL *The Metapheromenoi*
RAFAELA CONTRERAS *The Turquoise Ring and Other Stories*
ADOLFO COUVE *When I Think of My Missing Head*
QUENTIN S. CRISP *Aiaigasa*
LADY DILKE *The Outcast Spirit and Other Stories*
ÉDOUARD DUJARDIN *Hauntings*
BERIT ELLINGSEN *Now We Can See the Moon*
ERCKMANN-CHATRIAN *A Malediction*
ALPHONSE ESQUIROS *The Enchanted Castle*
ENRIQUE GÓMEZ CARRILLO *Sentimental Stories*
DELPHI FABRICE *The Red Spider*
EDMOND AND JULES DE GONCOURT *Manette Salomon*
REMY DE GOURMONT *From a Faraway Land*
REMY DE GOURMONT *Morose Vignettes*
GUIDO GOZZANO *Alcina and Other Stories*
GUSTAVE GUICHES *The Modesty of Sodom*
EDWARD HERON-ALLEN *The Complete Shorter Fiction*
EDWARD HERON-ALLEN *Three Ghost-Written Novels*
J.-K. HUYSMANS *The Crowds of Lourdes*
J.-K. HUYSMANS *Knapsacks*
COLIN INSOLE *Valerie and Other Stories*
JUSTIN ISIS *Pleasant Tales II*